W9-BHR-230

The Moonbow
of Mr. B. Bones

by J. Patrick Lewis
illustrated by Dirk Zimmer

Alfred A. Knopf ➤ New York

THIS IS A BORZOI BOOK
PUBLISHED BY ALFRED A. KNOPF, INC.
Text copyright © 1992 by J. Patrick Lewis
Illustrations copyright © 1992 by Dirk Zimmer
All rights reserved under International and Pan-American Copyright
Conventions. Published in the United States by Alfred A. Knopf, Inc.,
New York, and simultaneously in Canada by Random House of Canada
Limited, Toronto. Distributed by Random House, Inc., New York.
Book design by Elizabeth Hardie.   Manufactured in Singapore.

2   4   6   8   0   9   7   5   3

Library of Congress Cataloging-in-Publication Data
Lewis, J. Patrick. The moonbow of Mr. B. Bones / by J. Patrick
Lewis ; illustrated by Dirk Zimmer.   p.   cm. Summary: A new boy in a
small mountain village tries to discredit the old peddler who sells magic
jars of sundrops, moonbows, and the like; but though he drives the old
man away, something remarkable does happen in the sky.
ISBN 0-394-85365-2 ISBN 0-394-95365-7 (lib. bdg.)   [1. Peddlers
and peddling—Fiction. 2. Mountain life—Fiction.]
I. Zimmer, Dirk, ill. II. Title.   PZ7.L5866Mo
1992   E—dc19   88-37107

To Mick, Claudia & Brett,
and to Tim, Mary & Andy
J.P.L.

To Aram
D.Z.

In the middle of every Indian summer, an old man rode out of the mountains and into The Gap, a village lying deep in the bottomlands. Bartholomew Bones was his name, and he came with his mule and his wagon.

Little bits of everything filled that wagon: pumpkins and horseshoes, beeswax candles and foot-long matches, poem books and hand lotions, pots and pans and wooden spoons. And beneath the usual items lay what folks had waited all summer to see: a sackful of magic jars with mysterious labels—Sundrops, Snowrays, Moonbows, Rainflakes, and Whistling Wind.

From the barbershop to the fire station and all the houses in between,
The Gap was filled with the mountain man's jars. They were kept shiny
as ice and ready for show, and the magic was sealed in tight. Every boy
and girl bought them, and you could tell by their bulging pockets and fat
lunch bags that a peculiar kind of luck came from just carrying the jars
around.

But all that changed the year Tommy Morgan moved in.

On a June afternoon too hot to hurry, he sprang up from nowhere. Leaning against the old water pump, he twirled a yo-yo—a Silver Beauty with diamonds—into perfect loop-the-loops and cannonballs and backward round-the-worlds. Said he'd lived in a dozen towns up and down the mountains, and had seen just about everything there was worth seeing.

All that day and on through the summer, The Gap gang sat on the
drop edge of wonder listening to his stories.

A week or so the other side of Halloween, the wind let up and it got warm enough to sweat. Faithful as a grandfather's clock, Bartholomew Bones's wagon rumbled out of the woods. As he set up camp, girls and boys swarmed on him like molasses, welcoming him home.

All except Tommy, who stood back, taking big bites out of an apple, just waiting to make something happen.

"Whatcha sellin', Mister?" he asked, loud enough to quiet the commotion.

The old man looked the new boy over. "Depends on what you're buying," he said, and he turned away to sell his first Sundrops of the season to the Cawley twins.

"I'm interested in one of those secret weather bottles," Tommy butted in.

"What'll it be? Whistling Wind? Rainflakes?" said the old man, rummaging through his wagon.

Tommy shrugged his shoulders. "Any one of them'll do." Then he paid his ten cents and got himself a jar of Moonbows in return.

Jess Frye, Polly Hazlett, and the rest of The Gap gang were bunched up in line, eager to get new bottles. No one was ready for what happened next.

Tommy lay back in the grass close to the wagon and tilted his jar in the sunlight. He squinted his eyes nearly shut, but he couldn't see a thing inside. "I wonder what a Moonbow looks like," he said, running his finger over the label. "Is there liquid or powder in here? What's it s'posed to be?"

But he didn't wait for anybody to answer. "Maybe there ain't much glitter to the thing in daylight, anyway," he laughed to himself, and started to unfasten the lid.

The Gap went dead still.

Polly gulped air, and half a dozen
boys next to her went stiff as statues.

The old man waved his arms and was
about to yell something, but it was too
late.

12

Tommy snapped the wire back, and for the first time in the history of The Gap, the lid popped off one of Bartholomew Bones's magic jars!

13

Nothing came out.

Tommy peeked inside, smacked the bottom, shook it hard. Still nothing. And the quiet grew louder.

"It's empty!" Tommy shouted, though he didn't sound at all surprised. "Mister Beans or whatever-your-name-is, what d'you think you're selling here?"

The mountain man handed the boy his ten cents back. "Maybe you got a bad jar" was all he said.

Tommy looked up at the long line of bottle buyers. Jess pulled out his old Whistling Wind and rubbed it against his shirt. Polly stared hard at Tommy, then at the half-pints of the prize Rainflakes she held in each hand.

"Maybe they're *all* bad jars," said Tommy. He stuck the dime in his pocket, tossed the worthless bottle of Moonbows back in the wagon, and sauntered on home.

The rest of that day Mr. Bones sold only one ball of string, a honey dipper, and two good poem books. Instead of staying to trade stories with him, boys and girls suddenly remembered important chores and drifted away.

When The Gap was nearly deserted, the old man looked at his pocket watch, then shuffled down the red-brick street for the last time. "One jar of Moonbows left!" he shouted, stopping at each doorway. "On sale for a nickel, and it'll last a lifetime!" But by then nearly everyone pretended to be too busy to turn around. So Bartholomew Bones packed the wagon and led his mule out of The Gap.

Now Polly was sitting on her front porch when Mr. Bones rode past. Though the dark grew tall in the trees, she could see that he'd stopped his mule in the shadows by the waterfall. It looked like he was emptying a bottle into the creek. But Polly'd had enough mystery for one day, and she was tired. She rubbed her eyes and went inside.

18

Later that night, frost crawled up the windowpanes. True winter was in the air. The Gap had gone to sleep when a voice rang out near the edge of the woods. Houses lit up, windows and doors flew open.

There beside the woodpile was Polly, who'd gone out to get another
log for the stove.

"Look! Up there at the moon! Can you see it? It's a Moonbow.
A MOONBOW!" Her voice echoed down the hollow.

One by one, folks in nightgowns and pajamas leaned out of windows or shivered on the sidewalk, gawking at the sky. Nobody noticed the boy standing perfectly still at the foot of the waterfall. Bundled up in a blanket, he traced with his finger the curve of white light as it fell over the mountains.

24

Two hours later, when the street was quiet again and everyone else had gone back inside, the boy who said he'd seen everything that was worth seeing took one last look. Then Tommy Morgan bunched up his blanket and went home.

The old man never returned. But on certain nights ever since, The Gap fills up with folks from miles around, come to see what some call the Moonbow of Mr. B. Bones. When they ask what causes the strange white hoop of light, one boy tells the story best.

"There can be no fog or rain. Just the cool mist off the waterfall. A thousand stars are flying with the moon. And the sky," says Tommy Morgan, pointing up into the mountains, "the sky must be as clear as a glass jar."

J. Patrick Lewis is the author of critically acclaimed books for children, including *The Tsar & the Amazing Cow*, an original folk tale that, according to *The New York Times*, "deserves to become a classic"; *A Hippopotamusn't*, a collection of verse that received starred reviews from *School Library Journal*, *The Horn Book*, and *Booklist*; and, most recently, *Two-Legged, Four-Legged, No-Legged Rhymes* (Knopf).

After hearing tales of a strange light appearing in the night sky over Cumberland Falls, Kentucky, Mr. Lewis went to see for himself and was inspired to write this story. He lives in Westerville, Ohio, and teaches at Otterbein College.

Dirk Zimmer is the popular illustrator of many books for young readers, including *John Tabor's Ride*, by Edward C. Day, an IRA-CBC Teachers' Choice for 1990; and *The Adventures of Ratman*, by Ellen Weiss and Mel Friedman, an IRA-CBC Children's Choice for 1991. An illustrator with lots of kid appeal, Mr. Zimmer began drawing comic strips and making picture books when he was four years old.

He lives in Kingston, New York.

Author's Note
The moonbow is an actual natural phenomenon that appears under certain weather conditions at Cumberland Falls, Kentucky.